Tappety Tam Fairley

For Mam and Dad
Thanks for doing all of my odd jobs

First published in 2016 by
BC Books, an imprint of
Birlinn Limited
West Newington House
10 Newington Road
Edinburgh EH9 1QS

www.birlinn.co.uk

Text and illustrations copyright © Tim Archbold 2016

The moral right of Tim Archbold to be identified
as the author of this work has been asserted by him
in accordance with the Copyright, Designs and
Patents Act 1988

ISBN 978 1 78027 348 8

British Library Cataloguing-in-Publication Data
A catalogue record for this book is available from
the British Library

Typeset by Mark Blackadder

Printed and bound by Livonia Print, Latvia

Tappety Tam Fairley

Story and illustrations by Tim Archbold

This is a neat and tidy true story.
Do not drop litter, and please turn each page carefully.

Down a swept stone street,
around a neat grass green …

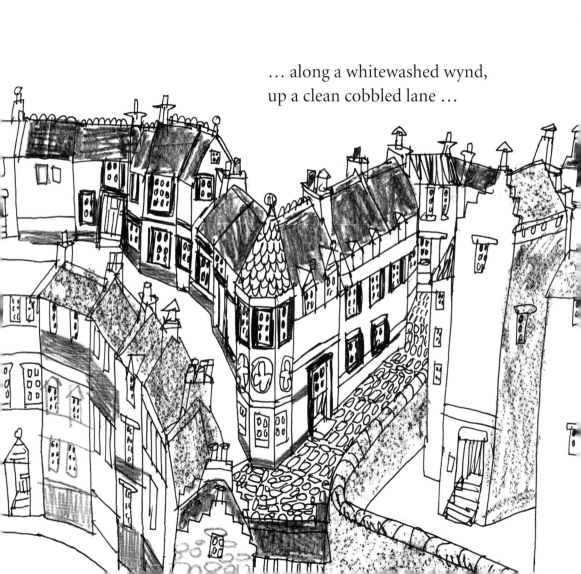

… along a whitewashed wynd,
up a clean cobbled lane …

... across a fine footbridge,
past a painted signpost ...

… through a new blue gate,
under a pruned plum tree …

… in a wee house of wood
lived Tappety Tam Fairley.

There was not an untidy cloud in the sky.

Tappety Tam was
an odd-job man.

(Now, you might be thinking, 'Today is a good day to plant potatoes,'
or, 'Are there are any biscuits left in the tin?' But also, just a little bit,
you are wondering, 'What is an odd job?' Well, it is any small, simple
job that you are too busy or too tired to do yourself. Your piano might
need moved from here to there. Your palace might need a coat of
paint, or you might have squeaky hinges.)

Tappety Tam could paint, polish, wash, weed, dig, drill, trim, tidy or make-do-and-mend just about anything.

Everything was perfect. Everything was peaceful.

Until the day of the **BEST KEPT VILLAGE COMPETITION**.

Tappety Tam lived in HighHope village, and with his help they had won First Prize every year.

Down the road a little way was LowHope village, and they had not won anything EVER. They were not pleased about this.

In HighHope village hall the important
Competition Committee met to make an
important list of odd jobs for Tappety Tam.

They had tea and cakes and chocolate
shortbread to eat.

'Cut the grass on the green and trim and tidy the scraggly old bushes,' suggested Lady Lavender-Bathwater.

Mrs Tiptoe-Loudly from the library said, 'Paint the village hall grey and brown.'

'Clean out the pond and fill it with fresh water,' cried Farmer Ferguson.

Captain McTrumpet said, 'Fill the street with flags and flowers.'

'Set out a tea table and chairs for three judges,' added Miss O'Dearie from the post office.

Captain McTrumpet signed the list on behalf of the HighHope Best Kept Village Competition Committee.

'Well done!' and 'That's it settled for another year!' and 'More tea, anyone?' they said.

BUT . . .

. . . there was one other person at the important meeting.

It was Mr Tallboy, who said he was the official Best Kept Village Competition inspector. Nobody had seen or heard of Mr Tallboy before, but he did have a badge, which read:

☆ Mr V. Tallboy ✸
offishyl Competishun
☆ Inspectr ✸✸✸

It had a lot of gold stars.

He also had a gold-topped pen and a briefcase.

He said he should inspect the list and
stamp it and sign it.

Mr Tallboy had eaten six cakes and eight
pieces of shortbread and he had drunk
four cups of very sugary tea.

He wiped his hands on his scarf and asked
if there was any more cake.

Mr Tallboy was, in fact, two small boys in
disguise. They were from LowHope village.
They had been sent to spy on HighHope
village and discover their plans and secrets.

(Look, I didn't make this up one wet
Wednesday afternoon. This is completely
true and I'm just telling you the story. Listen
carefully to the next bit – it's important.)

Mr Tallboy looked at the odd-job list. He waggled his big red moustache (it wasn't a real moustache) and slurped more sugary tea. A hand reached out from under his long coat and grabbed the last piece of shortbread. No one noticed.

Captain McTrumpet and Mrs Tiptoe-Loudly talked about the weather.

Lady Lavender-Bathwater talked about hats and Miss O'Dearie was showing Farmer Ferguson her sore knee.

They did not notice Mr Tallboy fold part of the list over and quickly make a few changes with his gold-topped pen.

The list of odd jobs now read:

1 Cut the grass on the green, and trim and tidy the scraggly old **people** ☆

2 Paint the village hall **red yellow blue spots stripes orange purple stars green**

3 Clean out the pond and fill it with **custard**

4 Fill the street with flags and flowers **and elephants**

5 Set out a tea table and chairs for three **hundred visitors**

Mr Tallboy stamped the list with a big inky stamp, which actually said, 'WAGGERS! Best dog biscuits', and added his twizzly signature.

MR. V. Tallboy

'Stamped and signed,' he said, with a shower of cake crumbs.

Captain McTrumpet popped the list into an envelope addressed to Tappety Tam, the odd-job man.

When it arrived the next day, Tam thought the list was a bit unusual, but it was stamped and signed by the committee, so it must be right.

The **BEST KEPT VILLAGE COMPETITION** judging was at four o'clock. Tam gathered his tools, paints and brushes, and set off on his bicycle.

THE VILLAGE GREEN

Tappety Tam soon cut and cleared the grass, but the old people did not want to be trimmed and tidied. Tam gently brushed their dusty hats and coats, polished their black boots and shoes, and trimmed wispy hair and wiry beards. He made buttons shine and dry old feathers stand up straight.

'We look great, Tam,' they giggled. 'But these old rose
bushes could do with a trim.'

Tappety Tam had already rushed off to the next job.

THE VILLAGE HALL

Tam sanded and cleaned the doors. He repaired the windows
and the woodwork. He filled up holes and brushed on primer.
He climbed his ladder and began to paint, first red then yellow,
blue, green, purple and orange, with spots, stripes and stars.

The village hall looked like a magnificent fireworks display. The children said, 'OOH!' and the children said, 'AAH!' and the children said they wanted their carts and bicycles painted the same.

Tappety Tam rushed off to the next job.

THE VILLAGE POND

Tam cleared the pond of old leaves, twigs and weeds. He caught the fish and frogs and placed them in a barrel of pond water for safekeeping.

Old Penny the grocer gave Tappety Tam three big boxes of Sunshine custard powder, and in exchange Tam painted the front of his shop green and gold.

With a little help, Tam mixed the custard powder
into the pond until it was thick and creamy.

The children rushed off to tell their friends
and Tappety Tam rushed off to the next job.

THE VILLAGE STREET

Granny Patch said she could make coloured flags for Tam if he would wash her windows. Bert Cooper said he had four empty barrels if Tam would paint his fence. Dusty Bluebell offered lots of flowers if Tam would clip her garden hedge.

Nobody in the street had an elephant. The children looked in sheds and outhouses but found nothing.

Mr Armstrong, the coalman, came along. He told Tam that his son was a sailor on a big ship and that he might know something about elephants because he had sailed all over the world. If Tam would paint his old cart, Mr Armstrong said he would go to the harbour and ask his sailor son about elephants.

Tappety Tam put the flags and flower barrels out along the street and then rushed off to the next job.

THE VILLAGE TEA

Hetty and Betty at the Tinkly Teacup offered to make all of the sandwiches, scones and cakes for the village tea. They wanted Tam to collect flour and butter and milk and eggs and cheese and ham.

At the flourmill, Mr McGill asked Tam to find his hat.

At the dairy, Miss Mary asked Tam to catch a rat.

Tam called at Trotters Farm for the ham.

He had to repair a dripping tap and then deliver bacon to Old Granny Tattle at Chatterbox Cottage, and she wanted a good gossip.

Tappety Tam returned to the village with the flour and butter and milk and eggs and cheese and ham and a letter to post for Old Granny Tattle.

He had to borrow tables, chairs and teapots. The tables all had wobbly legs, the chairs needed varnished and the teapots had to be glued.

But at four o'clock the judges arrived. Everything was ready . . . except the elephants.

The three judges walked through the village with notebooks and pencils ready. They looked at the green and said, 'Glorious!'

They looked at the trim and tidy old people, with their shiny shoes and fine feathery hats, and said, 'How do you do?'

The three judges looked at the scraggly old bushes and they scribbled in their notebooks.

They walked along the swept stone street and saw the village hall in fantastic firework colours. They saw bright painted bikes and carts and they saw a pond full of custard.

Children paddled in the custard, dogs and ducks swam about in the custard and everyone was eating pond custard. The three judges scribbled in their notebooks.

Along the street was a giant jumble of tables and chairs. Fresh scones, sponge cream cakes and sandwiches were set out on blue plates. Big brown teapots steamed. The three judges scribbled in their notebooks.

Suddenly, beyond the
flags and the flowers, at the end
of the street, an elephant appeared.

Two elephants. Three elephants walked trunk-to-tail.

Mr Armstrong followed in his cart with his sailor son and a beautiful Indian princess, who was on holiday.

The elephants carried everything she needed and also her two grandmas.

The cart was followed by a parade of
musicians and singing sailors.

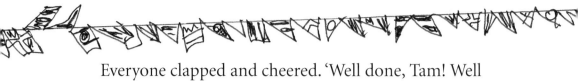

Everyone clapped and cheered. 'Well done, Tam! Well done!' they said, and everyone sat down for tea.

The three judges scribbled in their notebooks.

Mr Tallboy was already having tea and cake.

(Now, you are asking, 'Well? What happened?
Did they win? Did they win after all that fuss?')

Unfortunately, they did not win the
BEST KEPT VILLAGE COMPETITION.

Mrs Tiptoe-Loudly
danced with a
sailor.

An elephant
ate all of the flowers.

Miss O'Dearie slipped on
a buttered scone.

Lady Lavender-Bathwater's hat
was eaten by another elephant.

Farmer Ferguson was dunked
in the fish and frog barrel.

Captain McTrumpet was
thrown into the custard pond.

An elephant squirted the three judges with
custard and ate their notebooks. And . . .

. . . everyone ran home when it rained.

For the first time, to everyone's surprise, LowHope won the **BEST KEPT VILLAGE COMPETITION**. It was true because the certificate was stamped and signed by Mr V. Tallboy and it had a lot of gold stars.

('And what about Tam?' I hear you say. 'Poor Tappety Tam, what happened to him?' Don't worry, he was fine, because the beautiful Indian princess had asked him to be her odd-job man.

She said her piano needed moved from here to there. She said her palace needed a coat of paint and, she said, both her grandmas had squeaky hinges.)